VOICES FROM AROUND THE

PACIFIC ISLANDS

SĀMOA

Written by Jane Va'afusuaga

with Tuiafutea O. Va'afusuaga

NORWOOD HOUSE PRESS

Norwood House Press

For more information about Norwood House Press please visit our website at www.norwoodhousepress.com or call 866-565-2900.

Credits
Editor: Mari Bolte
Designer: Sara Radka

Photo Credits
page 3: ©Gil C / Shutterstock; page 4: ©Busakorn Pongparnit / Getty Images; page 4: ©John Sciulli / Staff / Getty Images; page 5: ©Dimitris66 / Getty Images; page 5: ©Peter Hermes Furian / Shutterstock; page 7: ©patrimonio designs ltd / Shutterstock; page 8: ©TSgt Hailey Haux / dvidshub.net; page 10: ©Thomas Andrew / Museum of New Zealand; page 11: ©Thomas Andrew / Museum of New Zealand; page 12: © / National Library of New Zealand; page 13: ©peacefoo / Shutterstock; page 14: ©Brandi Mueller / Getty Images; page 15: ©Ras Ras / Shutterstock; page 16: ©Fred Kruger / Newscom; page 17: ©Scott Barbour / Stringer / Getty Images; page 18: ©FastilyClone / Wikimedia; page 19: ©KOLI / Wikimedia; page 20: ©Teinesavaii / Wikimedia; page 21: ©Vaafusuaga Samalaulu Fonoti / Wikimedia; page 22: ©Peacefoo / Getty Images; page 23: ©KAVEBEAR / Wikimedia; page 25: ©Fotu Vaai / flickr.com; page 27: ©mvaligursky / Getty Images; page 27: ©Jamesafa3 / Wikimedia; page 28: ©bejdova / Shutterstock; page 29: ©corners74 / Shutterstock; page 30: ©Wainuiomartian / Wikimedia; page 31: ©worldtravel_photographer / Shutterstock; page 32: ©johan10 / Getty Images; page 33: ©Matt Roberts / Stringer / Getty Images; page 34: ©zstock / Shutterstock; page 35: ©corners74 / Shutterstock; page 36: ©Phil Walter / Staff / Getty Images; page 37: ©benoitb / Getty Images; page 38: ©Phil Walter / Staff / Getty Images; page 39: ©Hannah Peters / Staff / Getty Images; page 41: ©DouglasPeebles / DanitaDelimont.com / "Danita Delimont Photography" / Newscom; page 42: ©corners74 / Getty Images; page 43: ©Amy Sussman / Staff / Getty Images; page 44: ©Chris Jenner / Shutterstock; page 45: ©Shutterstock

Cover: ©nazar_ab / Getty Images; ©Kronocide~commonswiki / Wikimedia; ©imageBROKER/Michael Runkel / Getty Images

Library of Congress Cataloging-in-Publication Data
Names: Va'afusuaga, Jane, 1965- author. | Va'afusuaga, Tuiafutea O.
Title: Sāmoa / by Jane Va'afusuaga, with Tuiafutea O. Va'afusuaga.
Description: [Chicago] : Norwood House Press, [2023] | Series: Voices from around the world : Pacific islands | Includes index. | Audience: Ages 8-10 | Audience: Grades 4-6 | Summary: "The islands of Samoa are full of rich history and culture. Describes the history, customs, geography, and culture of the people who live there, and provides authentic vocabulary words for an immersive experience. Includes a glossary, index, and bibliography for further reading"-- Provided by publisher.
Identifiers: LCCN 2022025820 (print) | LCCN 2022025821 (ebook) | ISBN 9781684507474 (hardcover) | ISBN 9781684048144 (paperback) | ISBN 9781684048199 (epub)
Subjects: LCSH: Samoa--Juvenile literature.
Classification: LCC DU819.A2 V33 2022 (print) | LCC DU819.A2 (ebook) | DDC 996/.14--dc23/eng/20220601
LC record available at https://lccn.loc.gov/2022025820
LC ebook record available at https://lccn.loc.gov/2022025821

Hardcover ISBN: 978-1-68450-747-4
Paperback ISBN: 978-1-68404-814-4

Table of Contents

GUIDE TO SĀMOAN PRONUNCIATION

A (like car)
E (like egg)
I (like pick)
O (like hot)
U (like put)
G (like the *ng* in sing)

Welcome to
Sāmoa

Tālofa lava (hello) and *afio mai* (welcome)! The Sāmoans welcome you. They are the country's **indigenous** people. Three important concepts of their culture and life are love, family, and respect. Sāmoans welcome visitors by placing a sweet-smelling garland around their necks.

'Ava Ceremony

The *'ava ceremony* is an important part of Sāmoan culture. The 'ava ceremony is used to welcome visitors. It is also used to begin village meetings and other special events. 'Ava is a drink made by a young woman. She sits cross-legged in front of a *tanoa* (carved wooden bowl). She mixes the root of the 'ava plant with water. She uses fibers to strain the drink. A man serves the 'ava to *matai* (chiefs) and guests. They drink from a cup made from half a coconut shell.

People across the Pacific Islands take part in 'ava.

Where is Sāmoa?

Sāmoa is in the South Pacific Ocean. It is made up of a group of eight islands. The two largest islands are Savai'i and Upolu.

Apia is the capital of Sāmoa. It is also the only city.

SOUTH PACIFIC OCEAN

Savai'i

Apia

Upolu

SOUTH PACIFIC OCEAN

CHAPTER 1

The History of Sāmoa

Storytelling is a strength of the Sāmoan culture. Long before they were written down, Sāmoan myths and legends were spoken aloud. These stories kept the past alive. There may be different versions of the same tale.

There are many Sāmoan myths and legends about the god called Tagaloa. Also known as Tagaloa-lagi or Tagaloa of the heavens, he was the chief of all gods and the supreme ruler of Sāmoa. He lived in space and is credited with creating the universe.

The legend says that Tagaloa made nine heavens. He made the sky and the ocean. Next, he made the rivers and lakes. Then, he made land. Tagaloa threw two big stones down from heaven. One stone became the island of Savai'i. The other one became the island of Upolu.

DID YOU KNOW?

There are many versions of the meaning of the name *Sāmoa*. The most accepted one is that *Sā* means "sacred" and *moa* means "center," or "heart."

In other creation stories, Tagaloa's children take the shape of birds who look for land.

Tagaloa had a wife. They had two children. Their son was called Moa and their daughter was called Lu. Lu had a son, also called Lu. Tagaloa's grandson Lu argued with his uncle Moa. Then, he ran away to live on the islands called Sāmoa. Tagaloa sent a vine after him. Lu pulled up the vine. Its roots rotted and turned into worms. These worms became the first humans.

Throwing and catching, spinning, and dancing with nifo'oti showed off a dancer's skills. Fire was added later.

Sāmoa has many heritage items or cultural treasures. One is the *nifo'oti* (ceremonial knife). In the 19th century, whales were hunted in the Pacific Ocean. The whale hunters came ashore on the Sāmoan Islands to stock up on fresh drinking water, food, and firewood. They brought the metal whale knife to Sāmoa. Sāmoans included the hooked design of the whale knife into their war clubs.

Whether carved from wood or made from metal, nifoʻoti have a serrated edge and a hook on the end. The literal translation of nifoʻoti is "goat's horn." Goats were brought to Sāmoa about the same time as the whale knife. The knife's curved blade or hook resembled the goats' horns. Nifoʻoti have a cord braided from coconut fiber called sinnet. It is wrapped around the handle.

Today, carved wooden nifoʻoti are made as souvenirs. Nifoʻoti with a metal blade are ceremonial, and used for cultural dances. They are also used for fire dancing. Beginner dancers use one nifoʻoti. Both ends are wrapped in cloth and set on fire. Experienced dancers twirl two knives at the same time. They hook nifoʻoti together to make one long knife or twirl two knives at the same time.

Important Objects

Other heritage items of Sāmoa include the following:

- finely woven mats
- cloth made from the bark of the mulberry tree and painted with traditional designs
- carved wooden bowls for mixing ʻava
- **orator's** staff
- orator's fly whisk
- ceremonial headdresses worn by both men and women

Around 1000 BCE, seafarers from Southeast Asia left their homeland. They voyaged in double-hulled canoes with tall masts and woven sails. The seafarers navigated by the stars. They were skilled voyagers. Food like taro, breadfruit, and coconuts kept well for the long voyage. Chickens and pigs roamed the decks. The people reached the islands of Sāmoa between 1950 and 1500 BCE.

The people who came to Sāmoa most likely left their homeland to explore.

Sāmoans believe that their islands were the beginning point to great voyages. They believe **Polynesians** from there sailed to the east and south. This explains why Sāmoa is called the "heart" or "cradle" of Polynesia.

Around 950 CE, Tongan warriors arrived in Sāmoa. They came in large double-hulled canoes with sails that carried up to 100 men. In the 13th or 14th century, the Tongans were defeated in battle. They were chased out of Sāmoa by twin brothers called Tuna and Fata. The twins used wooden war clubs as their weapons. Sāmoa also had wars with Fiji. But there was also love between these Pacific islands. Members of the royal families intermarried.

Sāmoan canoes were fast and could change direction quickly. Building a canoe took many skilled workers and many resources.

Coconut oil was sold overseas to make soap and candles.

In 1722, Dutch explorer Jacob Roggeveen first saw the islands of Sāmoa. The French explorer Louis Antoine de Bougainville called Sāmoa "the Navigator Islands" in 1768. Soon, Europeans began to settle in Sāmoa. The first **missionaries** arrived around 1830.

By 1857, German merchant J. C. Godeffroy had set up the first European trading post in Sāmoa. Beachcombers came too. They were sailors who had been shipwrecked on the islands. Some of these early Europeans married Sāmoan women and had children.

Between 1889 and 1914, the country was colonized by Germany. Germans planted coconut, rubber, and cocoa. They built roads and bridges. Laborers from China and the Solomon Islands came in the early 1900s. They worked the plantations. These newcomers also married local women and had families.

In 1889, the famous Scottish author Robert Louis Stevenson came to live in Sāmoa. He is best known for his book *Treasure Island*. Stevenson built a house in Vailima. Today, that house is now a museum. When he died, the Sāmoans cut a path in the forest to bury him at the top of Mount Vaea. This is a popular hiking trail today for locals and tourists.

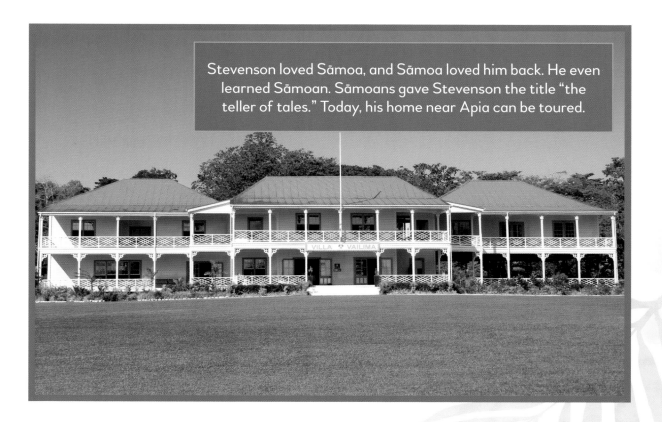

Stevenson loved Sāmoa, and Sāmoa loved him back. He even learned Sāmoan. Sāmoans gave Stevenson the title "the teller of tales." Today, his home near Apia can be toured.

Sāmoa is a group of eight islands in the South Pacific Ocean. The biggest island is Savai'i. The highest point in Sāmoa is there. It is called Mount Silisili and is 6,096 feet (1,858 meters) tall.

Hundreds of coral reefs surround the islands of Sāmoa.

The other large island is Upolu. They both have volcanoes. The capital city, Apia, is on Upolu. Manono and Apolima are smaller. The islands of Nu'utele, Nu'ulua, Fanuatapu, and Namua are even tinier. Nobody lives on them. In 2022, the population was just over 200,000 people. Around 40,000 people live in Apia. Most families live in villages near the coast.

American Sāmoa is a separate group of islands. It is 102 miles (164 kilometers) away and is governed by the United States. The capital city of American Sāmoa is called Pago Pago.

There are two main seasons in Sāmoa. The dry season is from May to October. The wet season is from November to April. This is when most **cyclones** happen. Sāmoa is 13 degrees below Earth's **equator**. This means it is warm year-round. The average temperatures range between 75 to 86 degrees Fahrenheit (24 to 30 degrees Celsius).

Fuipisia is a 180-foot (55-m)-tall waterfall near Apia.

CHAPTER 2

Sāmoan Culture

Sāmoa's motto is "*Fa'avae Sāmoa i le Atua.*" This means "Sāmoa is founded on God." In early times, Sāmoans worshipped the god Tagaloa. They first became aware of Christianity through contact with other Pacific Islands like Fiji and Tonga.

Food, church services, gatherings, and performances are part of White Sunday.

DID YOU KNOW?

In villages, a conch shell is blown each evening at sunset.
This lets people know it is time for family prayers.

In 1830, a missionary named John Williams arrived in Savai'i. He was from the London Missionary Society (LMS). He brought a team of eight others from Tahiti and Fiji. Sāmoans accepted this new religion. There were many aspects that were familiar to what they already believed. Christianity spread quickly throughout the country.

Choir groups are invited to sing during festivals and important events.

Today, Christianity plays a big part in the Sāmoan culture. Sunday is observed as a day of rest. Most businesses are closed. No sports are played. Most Sāmoan families attend church on Sunday mornings. People wear white clothes and hats to church. Many churches have large choirs or worship bands. Extended families share a traditional lunch after church.

Children's Day, also called White Sunday, is in October. It is also celebrated at church. Mother's Day and Father's Day are church activities as well. Today, every village has at least one church.

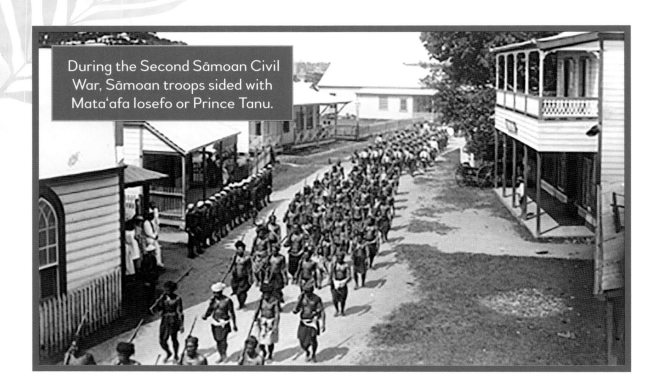

During the Second Sāmoan Civil War, Sāmoan troops sided with Mataʻafa Iosefo or Prince Tanu.

Many historical and cultural events have shaped Sāmoa's history. The first civil war took place between 1886 and 1894. Malietoa Laupepa and Mataʻafa Iosefo fought over who would be king. Germany, the United Kingdom, and the United States were also involved in the conflict. They all wanted to rule Sāmoa. Their involvement led to the Sāmoan Crisis. As the war ended, it was agreed that Malietoa Laupepa would be king of Sāmoa.

In 1898, Malietoa Laupepa died. A second civil war began. The United States, Germany, and the United Kingdom were involved once more. This war ended in 1899. Germany would rule Sāmoa. American Sāmoa would become a territory of the United States. It was agreed that Sāmoa would keep its customs and traditions.

From 1905 to 1911, Mount Matavanu erupted. Five villages were buried under a lava flow that covered 19.3 square miles (50 square kilometers). The people in the nearby villages were relocated to villages in Upolu. Today, this area is called the Saleaula lava field.

In 1918, the ship SS *Talune* left New Zealand. There were sick sailors on board. When it reached Apia, it started an **influenza epidemic**. Sadly, one quarter of Sāmoa's population died.

In 2002, the prime minister of New Zealand apologized to the Sāmoan people for allowing sick passengers to get off the SS *Talune* in Sāmoa.

The Mau was formed in 1908. It was a peaceful protest movement. They wanted independence. It was supported by the majority of Sāmoans. Sāmoa was governed by New Zealand after World War I (1914–1918). The Mau didn't agree with some of the new laws. The powers of the matai were being lessened.

Black Saturday will always be remembered as a sad day in the country's history. It took place on December 28, 1929, during a peaceful protest. The leader of the Mau movement, Tupua Tamasese Lealofi III, was killed. He was shot by the New Zealand police. Eight other people also died that day.

The Women's Mau movement sang, danced, and marched in protest, even though those activities were banned.

On January 1, 1962, Sāmoa finally gained Independence from New Zealand. The flag was raised in a ceremony at Mulinuʻu. Two heads of state were appointed. Their names were Tupua Tamasese Meaole and Malietoa Tanumafili II. Meaole died the next year. Tanumafili remained as the only head of state for 45 years until his death in 2007.

The country's first prime minister was Fiamē Mataʻafa Faumuina Mulinuʻu II. He was in office from 1960 until 1970. He was re-elected in 1973 and served until his death in 1975. In 2021, his daughter, Fiamē Naomi Mataʻafa, became the first female prime minister.

Tupua Tamasese Meaole (left) and Malietoa Tanumafili II raise the Sāmoan flag on the country's first Independence Day.

DID YOU KNOW?

Sāmoa was known as Western Sāmoa until 1997. Then, it was changed to the Independent Republic of Sāmoa, or just Sāmoa.

Meeting houses are used for meetings, gatherings, and other important events.

Each 'āiga (extended family) has its own matai titles. These titles relate to districts, villages, or land. Men and women are chosen to be matai by their 'āiga. Matai may be high chiefs or orators. The person who holds the highest title of the highest ranked family in the village is called the paramount chief.

Matai titles are given in a special ceremony. 'Ava is served to each matai as their new names are called out. The matai is called by this new name from that day on. Each village has an oral history of their matai titles and ranks. A person may hold more than one matai title. They may hold titles from both sides of their family. They may also be given a title from their husband or wife's family.

The role of the matai is to represent their 'āiga at village meetings. These are held in every village every month. All matai attend. They sit cross-legged in order of their rank. The paramount chief sits at the head of the meeting while village laws are discussed.

Only matai can be elected to parliament. The current prime minister of Sāmoa, Fiamē Naomi Mata'afa, holds the Fiamē title from Lotofaga village. Her father held the same title before her. He also held two other chiefly titles (Mata'afa and Faumuina). Each title has its own rank and importance.

The original Parliament House at Mulinu'u was built in 1916. It was rebuilt and modernized in 2019.

The art of tattooing is a significant part of many Pacific cultures. There is a Sāmoan legend about two women from Fiji who swam to Sāmoa. They brought tattooing tools along. They were singing, "Tattoo the women and not the men." Then, they got their words mixed up and sang, "Tattoo the men and not the women." Today, both men and women in Sāmoa are tattooed.

Receiving a traditional tattoo is a **rite of passage** to manhood. It is traditionally worn by matai. The male tattoo covers most of the lower part of a man's body. It reaches from the navel to just past the knees.

Women also have a traditional tattoo. This tattoo covers a woman's legs from her thighs to just below her knees. It is not as dense as the men's tattoo. Traditionally, the tattoo is worn by the daughter of a high chief. Her tattoo is usually hidden under her clothes, except if she is dancing. Then, she proudly shows it off.

Sāmoan Symbols

Sāmoan tattoos have importance to the people who receive them. Some designs, like the ones here, are meaningful to women.

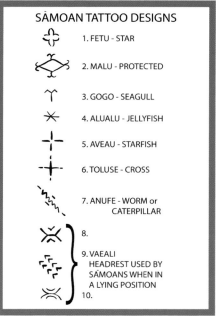

SĀMOAN TATTOO DESIGNS

1. FETU - STAR
2. MALU - PROTECTED
3. GOGO - SEAGULL
4. ALUALU - JELLYFISH
5. AVEAU - STARFISH
6. TOLUSE - CROSS
7. ANUFE - WORM or CATERPILLAR
8.
9. VAEALI HEADREST USED BY SĀMOANS WHEN IN A LYING POSITION
10.

Sāmoan tattoos are unique and full of meaning.

Sāmoans love celebrations! White Sunday is a very special day for children. They are given new white clothes to wear to church. Then, they recite Bible verses, sing songs, dance, and take part in plays. After church, there is a feast of Sāmoan food and ice cream.

Independence celebrations are held on June 1. A parade in Apia is led by the police band. The Sāmoan flag is raised at the parliament grounds. Groups of people from government departments, organizations, and schools march behind the police band. They salute and wave to important people like the head of state and the prime minister. After the parade, there is cultural dancing and entertainment.

A Race to the Finish

Longboat races are held during both Independence and Teuila celebrations. The boats represent different villages. It's always a fierce competition. Each boat has a crew of 48 rowers. Vaimasenu'u Zita Martel was the first woman captain. In 2006, her boat, *Segavao*, won a race in American Sāmoa. In 2020, she chose an all-women crew to race in a boat called *Fautasi o Toa*. They won the Marist St. Joseph's 70th Jubilee Race.

The Teuila Festival has been held in the first week of September since 1991. *Teuila* (torch ginger) is the national flower of Sāmoa. The Teuila Festival is a weeklong celebration of Sāmoan culture organized by the Sāmoa Tourism Authority. There are sports and singing and dancing competitions. Market stalls sell crafts and food. The festival attracts locals and visitors from overseas.

The seeds, leaves, and flowers of teuila are edible.

The Miss Sāmoa Pageant is held during the Teuila Festival. The winner receives a crown and a sash. She represents Sāmoa at the Miss South Pacific Pageant.

A Miss Sāmoa has been crowned every year since 1986.

CHAPTER 3

Sāmoa Today

Sāmoans are proud of their language and culture. They keep it alive through songs, dances, books, TV shows, and church services.

Some families in Sāmoa live in houses without walls. Others live in enclosed houses. Many have a *talimalo*. This is another large open house. It is used for family or village meetings. Guests and visitors stay there.

Talimalo are houses without walls. This lets cool air in during meetings or gatherings.

Many families in Sāmoan villages live a **subsistence** lifestyle. They grow coconuts, bananas, taro, and other crops. They also raise chickens and pigs. Their main sources of income are from selling crops or fishing. Some family members might work as teachers or in an office in Apia. Family members living overseas send money to help those back home.

Local fish and produce markets can be found across Sāmoa.

In the village, food is usually prepared over the fire in an open cookhouse. On Sundays, a traditional feast is prepared. Men cook food on hot rocks in an above-ground oven. Baked taro, breadfruit, young taro leaves cooked in coconut cream, chicken, fish, and roasted pig are commonly served. Sunday lunch is enjoyed by the whole 'āiga.

Not everyone lives in a village. Apia is a bustling city with many cars, shops, government offices, businesses, restaurants, and cafés. Most people who stay in town live in European-style houses. *Lavalava* are 6 feet (2 yards) of colorful material wrapped around the waist. Lavalava are worn every day by Sāmoans around the house and to do chores. Women wear a two-piece formal garment. It has a top and a long wraparound skirt. Formal wear for men is an island-style shirt and a colored wraparound skirt.

Formal dresses are worn for many special occasions, including public or school events.

DID YOU KNOW?

Having more visitors to Apia is changing other parts of Sāmoan life too. In 2009, the Sāmoan government changed the side of the road cars drove on. Sāmoans used to drive on the right side of the road. The driver was on the left side of the car. But now, the driver is on the right and the driving lane is on the left. Doing this made getting around easier for tourists from Austrlia and New Zealand.

Unique and colorful buses wait to take travelers around Apia.

Colorful buses travel between Apia and each village. Riders find a seat. They pay when they get off. If the bus is full, people sit on each other's laps.

Modern technology has found the island nation. In 2007, cell phones were introduced all over Sāmoa. This made it easier to stay in touch with family and friends. It also gave more people access to the internet.

Sāmoan dollars are called tala. The currency symbol is WST$.

Clothes and buses aren't the only colorful things in Sāmoa. The houses are painted in bright shades. School children wear colorful uniforms. They usually match their school building. Coworkers like to dress alike in patterned clothes. Even Sāmoan money is colorful. Pictures of famous people, famous places, and nature are printed in every color across the bills. Sāmoan dollar bills have been called the most beautiful money in the world.

The islands are full of natural color too. Along the coast, there are green palm trees, white sand, and blue sea. Inland is lush and green. A competition is held every year to choose the most beautiful village. There are gardens full of flowers and colorful plants.

The Sāmoan flag is red and blue. Red represents bravery. Blue represents freedom. The Southern Cross **constellation** is shown as five white stars over the blue. White represents purity. The flag is raised every morning in front of the government building by the police.

UFC fighter Mark Hunt (left) and rugby players Josh McGuire and Anthony Milford pose with the Sāmoan flag.

The economy is dependent on tourism. Resort workers, café staff, taxi drivers, and rental car clerks are common jobs. Some people make and sell handicrafts for tourists.

There are lots of things for visitors to do in Sāmoa. Sleeping overnight in a *fale* (house) at the beach or watching fire dancers twirl nifoʻoti are popular. Some people like to snorkel, hike in the rain forest, or visit a waterfall.

In 2019, more than 150,000 tourists visited Sāmoa.

Tourists love to sample delicious Sāmoan food too. Fresh fish and seafood are often found on the menu. Breadfruit, taro leaves, or roasted pig are things most tourists don't get at home. Market stalls sell freshly picked vegetables and fresh fruit like mangoes, pineapple, bananas, and papaya. Coconut trees are called the "tree of life." They provide food, fuel, building materials, medicine, cosmetics, and more.

Artisans sell beautiful crafts. But Sāmoa's many tropical flowers don't require any extra craftwork. They are beautiful on their own. Sāmoan women like to wear a flower in their hair.

A popular Sāmoan dish is raw fish marinated in coconut cream. It can be made with tuna or any white fish.

Seeing Sāmoa

Want to visit Sāmoa? Here are some things for visitors to remember:

- Sunday is a day of rest. Most tourist attractions will be closed.
- Dress modestly in church and in the villages.
- Take off your shoes before entering a house.
- Don't stand if elders are sitting.
- Sit cross-legged inside a fale and wear a lavalava. Don't point your feet at anyone.

The tsunami in 2009 caused widespread damage and loss of life.

Sāmoa has suffered several natural disasters. In the early 1990s, Cyclones Ofa and Val caused severe damage to houses, buildings, and crops. In 2012, Cyclone Evan caused more destruction. Around 4,500 people had to seek emergency shelter. Many crops, such as bananas, breadfruit, and coconuts, were damaged or destroyed.

On September 29, 2009, two large earthquakes struck between Sāmoa and American Sāmoa. The earthquakes generated a **tsunami**. Waves higher than 72 feet (22 m) hit the southeast side of Upolu. Homes were lost. Many people were injured. In Sāmoa, 149 people died, and another 34 died in American Sāmoa.

Sāmoans worked hard to rebuild their houses and replant crops. Countries like the United States, China, Australia, and New Zealand helped with the rebuilding.

Like many Pacific Islands, Samoa is affected by **climate change**. Low-lying villages are prone to rising sea levels. Coastal areas are being worn away. There are many conservation projects with the islands' health in mind. Thousands of trees are being planted in the rain forests. Mangrove forests are being restored, and many areas are being set up for conservation.

The national bird of Sāmoa, the tooth-billed pigeon, also known as the manumea, is almost extinct. There is a campaign to save the pigeon and other native birds. These conservation efforts help to improve the environment for the next generation of Sāmoans to enjoy.

The manumea eats fruit, seeds, and plants. Its unique orange bill has toothlike tips on the top and bottom.

Ele Opeloge comes from a family of internationally recognized weightlifters.

Sāmoans love to play sports. Rugby, netball, volleyball, cricket, weightlifting, and boxing are popular. Sāmoans have both 7- and 15-player rugby teams. Before each game, the players perform a battle dance called *siva tau*. It is a challenge to the other team. The Rugby Sevens won the 2009–10 World Series.

Sāmoa has competed in the Olympic Games since 1984. In 2008, Ele Opeloge won Sāmoa's first Olympic medal in weightlifting. She was awarded a silver medal. In 2021, 11 athletes represented the country at the Tokyo Summer Olympics. Sāmoa has never participated in a Winter Olympics.

Cricket is played across Sāmoa. There are two versions of the game. Sāmoan cricket is played with teams of up to 50 people. The wooden bat is a triangular shape wrapped with sinnet. English cricket is played with 11 players on each side.

Rugby in Sāmoa

In 1924, a religious organization called the Marist Brothers brought the game of rugby to Western Sāmoa. Today, rugby is the national sport of Sāmoa. It is played by both men and women.

The men's team is called the Manu Sāmoa, after a famous warrior. The 15-aside team famously beat Wales 16–13 during the 1991 Rugby World Cup.

The women's team is called Manu Sina. They first played in 2000. The men's and women's rugby teams include local and overseas players. The teams wear blue jerseys and white shorts.

Music and art are part of the country's culture. Sāmoans grow up singing in the church choir.

Children are taught cultural dancing at school, at church, and at home. Cultural dance competitions are held at all major celebrations. There is great rivalry between groups and villages. Traditional, gospel, and modern hip-hop are all popular in Sāmoa.

Electronic piano, guitar, and ukulele are common instruments. Drums are used for cultural dancing and fire dancing. Some bands start out playing at resorts. They can become popular all around Sāmoa. Jerome Grey is a well-known singer. He wrote the song "We Are Sāmoa." In 2021, he was named the Polynesian Artist of the Decade.

Richard Parker and Lolenese Usoali'i are well-known Sāmoan singers and songwriters. They live in the islands. Other famous Sāmoan musicians live overseas.

There is a fine art school in Sāmoa that produces many talented artists. The students have a reputation for skillful painting and wood carving. Manamea is an art studio in Apia. Their artists create modern art and carvings.

Traditional Sāmoan instruments include a drum made from a hollow log and a rolled mat that is beaten with sticks.

Sāmoans living overseas can be dual citizens. They can hold citizenship in Sāmoa and in the country where they live.

Since the 1950s, Sāmoans have migrated all over the world. Recently, many Sāmoans and other Pacific Islanders have left their islands. Most of them have gone to New Zealand and Australia to pick fruit. They save their wages and send money back to their families in the islands. Others are awarded scholarships to study overseas. Once they are done with school, they return to work in Sāmoa.

DID YOU KNOW?

There are more than twice as many Sāmoans living overseas as there are living on the islands. Around 500,000 Sāmoans live overseas. They are found mainly in the United States, Australia, and New Zealand.

Many Sāmoan families living overseas have kept strong ties with their homeland. They return to their island home to visit family and connect with their roots. They may go back to Sāmoa for a vacation or to attend a funeral or a wedding. Other reasons might be to celebrate White Sunday, Independence, or to attend a matai bestowal ceremony.

Some Famous Sāmoans

Sāmoans have made their mark around the world. Here are a few of the most famous, and where they settled.

- Seiuli Dwayne "The Rock" Johnson (United States) - actor

- David Tua (New Zealand) - boxer

- Albert Wendt (New Zealand) - author

- Selina Tusitala Marsh (New Zealand) - poet

- Adeaze (New Zealand) - musicians

- Sir Michael Jones (New Zealand) - rugby player

Seiuli Dwayne Johnson

CHAPTER 4

A Blend of the Old and the New

If you visit Sāmoa today, you will discover that it's a blend of the old and the new. Village life is more traditional and laid back. Many families grow their own crops. Fishermen feed their families from the ocean. Colorful buses carry passengers into town every day. Life in Apia is busy with lots of traffic, modern buildings, and fast-food restaurants. English and Sāmoan words are spoken.

The capital city of Apia is a blend of traditional and modern design.

You're Calling When?

In 2011, Sāmoa skipped December 31. This moved the country across the **international date line**. This change is to make it easier to do business with countries like New Zealand. Before this change, Sāmoa was a whole day behind New Zealand. This caused confusion for flight arrivals and departures. It meant there were only three days in the middle of the week for business to be done.

Russia

United States

Sāmoa

Australia

Many Sāmoan heritage items are still in use today. The nifoʻoti is used for cultural dancing and fire dancing. Headdresses are worn by dancers. Women weave fine mats that are exchanged at weddings and funerals. ʻAva ceremonies begin meetings and welcome guests. An orator or talking chief will use his staff or fly whisk to speak. Ceremonies are held to bestow new matai titles.

The Sāmoan culture has been valued and built upon. Whether it's a centuries-old tradition or a modern twist to a classic, Sāmoans show how a society can grow independently.

Sāmoan Glossary

Remember to check page 3 for tips on pronunciation!

afio mai: welcome

'āiga: extended family

'ava ceremony: a ceremony that involves mixing the roots of the 'ava plant with water to make a drink; also known as kava

fale: house

fa'avae samoa ile atha: the motto of Sāmoa

lavalava: a rectangular piece of cloth worn like a wraparound skirt

matai: chief

moa: center or heart

nifo'oti: ceremonial knife with a serrated edge and a hook on the end; they are used for cultural dancing and fire dancing

sā: sacred

sīva tau: battle dance performed by the Manu Sāmoa rugby team

talimalo: large meeting house that is round, oval, or rectangular in shape; it has no wall, and the roof is held up by strong poles

tālofa lava: hello

tanoa: carved wooden bowl

teuila: torch ginger, the national flower of Sāmoa

English Glossary

climate change (CLY-muht CHAYNJ): long-term shifts in temperatures and weather patterns

constellation (kahn-stuh-LAY-shuhn): a group of stars that form a recognizable pattern

cyclones (SY-klohns): a system of rotating winds that forms over tropical water; also known as hurricanes or typhoons

equator (EE-kway-tuhr): an imaginary line around the middle of Earth that divides it in half

indigenous (in-DIJ-uh-nuss): native to an area

influenza epidemic (in-floo-EN-zuh ep-uh-DEM-ik): a global outbreak of a deadly influenza virus

international date line (IN-tuhr-nash-uh-nuhl DAYT LINE): an invisible line that runs from the North Pole to the South Pole; it serves as the boundary between one calendar day and the next

missionaries (MISH-uh-nehr-ees): people sent to promote Christianity in a foreign country

orators (OHR-ay-tuhrz): people who speak

Polynesians (pah-luh-NEE-zee-unz): the indigenous people of the Pacific Island

rite of passage (RYT of PASS-uhj): a ritual or event that marks a change in a person's life

subsistence (sub-SIS-tuhnz): farming enough crops for your family

tsunami (SOO-nah-mee): a series of waves caused by earthquakes, volcanic eruptions, and other underwater explosions

Read More about the Pacific Islands

Books

Doeden, Matt. *Travel to Australia.* Minneapolis, MN: Lerner Publications, 2022.

Toumuʻa, M. Ruth. *Tonga.* Chicago, IL: Norwood House Press, 2023.

Websites

Kids: Britannica (https://kids.britannica.com/kids/article/Samoa/346206) Learn about Sāmoa, the people who live there, and more.

Wellington City Libraries: Kids Blog (https://www.wcl.govt.nz/blogs/kids/index.php/tag/samoa/) Book resources, language lessons, and kid-friendly resources about Sāmoa.

Index

About the Author

Jane Vaʻafusuaga was born and raised in New Zealand. She has lived in Sāmoa for 20 years. Jane and her husband have an ecotourism business and work on various conservation projects. She writes books for children.

About the Consultant

Tuiafutea Olsen Vaʻafusuaga (Faleaseʻela, Tuanaʻi, Tanugamanono, Taga) is of Sāmoan heritage. He was born and raised in New Zealand. He has lived in Sāmoa for over 30 years and is a high chief of the village of Faleaseʻela. Tuiafutea runs an ecotourism business and is the project manager for the Faleaseʻela Environment Protection Society (FEPS).